For Mom, who would've known Jerry was special right from the start.—L.G.S.

In loving memory of George Langberg, a great uncle with a very green thumb.—A.V.

For my tatay, Norberto, a loving and nurturing father.—L.B.

G. P. PUTNAM'S SONS

An imprint of Penguin Random House LLC, New York

First published in the United States of America by G. P. Putnam's Sons, an imprint of Penguin Random House LLC, 2023

Text copyright © 2023 by Elizabeth Garton Scanlon and Audrey Vernick
Illustrations copyright © 2023 by Lynnor Bontigao

G. P. Putnam's Sons is a registered trademark of Penguin Random House LLC.

The Penguin colophon is a registered trademark of Penguin Books Limited.

Visit us online at penguinrandomhouse.com.

Library of Congress Cataloging-in-Publication Data
Names: Scanlon, Liz Garton, author. | Vernick, Audrey, author. | Bontigao, Lynnor, illustrator.
Title: The world's best class plant / Liz Garton Scanlon and Audrey Vernick; illustrated by Lynnor Bontigao.
Description: New York: G. P. Putnam's Sons, 2023. | Summary: A class that is terribly disappointed in their lack of a class pet discovers that having a class plant is the best thing ever.
Identifiers: LCCN 2021053553 (print) | LCCN 2021053554 (ebook) | ISBN 9780525516354 (hardcover) | ISBN 9780525516385 (kindle edition) | ISBN 9780525516361 (epub)
Subjects: CYAC: Plants—Fiction. | Schools—Fiction. | Pets—Fiction. | LCGFT: Picture books.
Classification: LCC PZ7.1.S32 Wo 2023 (print) | LCC PZ7.1.S32 (ebook) | DDC [E]—dc23
LC record available at https://lccn.loc.gov/2021053553
LC ebook record available at https://lccn.loc.gov/2021053554

Manufactured in China

ISBN 9780525516354

1 3 5 7 9 10 8 6 4 2

TOPL

Design by Marikka Tamura | Text set in Rockwell
The art was created digitally.

The WORLD'S BEST CLASS PLANT

LIZ GARTON SCANLON AND AUDREY VERNICK

ILLUSTRATED BY LYNNOR BONTIGAO

putnam

G. P. PUTNAM'S SONS

Room 107 has a cockatiel.

Room 108 has a chinchilla.

Even the Art Room has
a bearded dragon!

But in Room 109, Arlo's classroom, there is a plant.

A mostly green, hardly growing, never moving plant.

Instead of doing fun class-pet stuff—shredding the newspaper bedding,

filling the food bowl,

cradling the creature carefully and passing it around their morning circle—

Arlo's class takes turns watering.

Sometimes they forget,
because it doesn't squeak
or whistle or whimper.

It's just a plant.

Mr. Boring (not his real name) says the plant is "more than enough excitement for us."

Arlo thinks Mr. Boring doesn't know what *excitement* means, because this plant is about as exciting as a thumbtack. Or cornflakes. Or the sidewalk.

Arlo *wishes* it was exciting. He wishes Room 109 had a silly but trusty companion instead of a blob in a plastic pot on the windowsill. He wishes for someone to hold and whisper secrets to and love.

One morning, Arlo raises his hand and announces,

Otis barely gets his suggestion out before
Mr. Bummer (not his real name) says,

Arlo opens his mouth to protest, but when he
looks at the plant, he realizes Mr. Bummer is right.
That plant *is* Jerry. Everyone agrees.

Something about *naming* the blob makes it more exciting.

All of Room 109 rushes over to sing Jerry's praises
and add jobs to the chore chart:

BRING JERRY HOME FOR THE WEEKEND
SWEEP UP DROPPED LEAVES
TURN JERRY TOWARD THE LIGHT

As the days pass, strange things happen.
Jerry gets . . .

greener.

And longer.

And twistier.

In fact, Jerry gets so green
and long and twisty that he
outgrows his plastic pot.

POTTING MIX

Kids come to school bursting with the stuff they've learned.
Like, it turns out Jerry is a spider plant!
And if you water him too much, you can kill him!
And—this is unbelievable—Jerry makes little baby Jerrys.
They're called spiderettes!
You can cut them off and they'll turn into whole new plants.
(Don't try that with a cockatiel or chinchilla.)

One morning, when it's Arlo's job to do the misting,
he's pretty sure he hears Jerry breathe.
No, not breathe. More like . . . whisper.

"I know, Jerry," Arlo whispers back.
"Everybody likes feeling special."

When Room 109 asks if they can have a Jerry Appreciation Day,
Mr. Patient (not his real name) says yes. Talk about exciting!
They plan leafy costumes! Green snacks! Watering can races!

Word spreads, of course.

The kids from Room 107 ask to trade their cockatiel for Jerry.

NO WAY!

Room 108 wants their chinchilla to meet Jerry.

(What if the chinchilla EATS Jerry?)

NO WAY!

Everyone wants to come
to Jerry Appreciation Day.

"Everyone *should* get to know Jerry," says Mia.
"With his fine green leaves . . ."
"And surprising twists," say Sylvie and Levar.

"And . . . just his . . ." Arlo reaches his arms out wide—
there are no words to express the greatness of Jerry.

So Jerry Appreciation Day goes schoolwide.

It's glorious and spectacular and joyous, but wow,
the kids in Room 109 are whooped by the end. Jerry
really *is* as much excitement as they can handle.

They're relieved when everyone goes back to their classrooms and they have Jerry to themselves again.

For the rest of the year,
they mist and fluff and turn
and love their class plant.

Then, on the last day of school, when it's time to say goodbye to Jerry, Mr. Perfect (*should* be his real name) says, "You each get to bring home a baby Jerry of your very own."

When Arlo's next-year teacher, Ms. No-Nonsense (not her real name), offers up a rock as the class pet, Arlo remembers how Jerry used to be a mostly green, hardly growing, never moving plant—before Mr. Smart (actually his real name) let them name him.

So Arlo picks up the rock
and examines it closely.

He turns it over

and feels the weight
of it in his hands.

He really gets to know it before whispering quietly,
"Brenda? Is that you?"

So You're Ready to Raise a Plant of Your Own . . .

Not every plant can have the greatness of Jerry, but even ordinary plants can provide you with a whole lot of love and nature! Plus, you might learn a thing or two about seeds and roots and stems and soil as you care for your new green pal.

Just as you wouldn't put a penguin in the desert (unless you were writing a *fantastic* story), you wouldn't want to put a cactus, say, in the rain forest. Some plants need more sun. Others need a lot of water. And still others are always outgrowing their pots! Which one is right for you?

Now, don't let the science-y names of these kid-friendly plants scare you. Some people call *Dracaena sanderiana* **lucky bamboo**, and who couldn't use a little extra luck?

Pilea peperomioides is also called the **friendship plant**; just like Jerry with his spiderettes, the friendship plant grows babies, or "pups."

Another good plant is *Ficus lyrata*, which is better known by the fun-to-say name **fiddle-leaf fig**.

Make sure you learn how to take care of the plant you choose. Watering or misting? Full sun or partial shade? Keep the soil moist or let it dry out between waterings? It's simple to keep your plant happy and thriving as long as you understand what it needs.

Of course, you can't go wrong with a **spider plant** (*Chlorophytum comosum*). Just make sure that you pick the perfect name.